OUTSIDE

By Joseph S. Bonsall

Illustrated by Erin Marie Mauterer

Ideals Children's Books • Nashville, Tennessee
an imprint of Hambleton-Hill Publishing, Inc.

To my wonderful parents, Joe and Lillie Bonsall; my sister Nancy; my loving
wife, Mary Ann; my beautiful daughters, Jennifer and Sabrina; and my
biggest Molly Book fan, granddaughter Breane.
Also to Snuggles (the real Spooker), Sealy Blue, Harrah, and The Dude. Rest
well in The Better Place sweet kitties!

—J. S. B.

For my girls, Madelyn and Marguerite.
There is so much for you outside in this big, wide world!

—Mommy

Published by Ideals Children's Books
An imprint of Hambleton-Hill Publishing, Inc.
Nashville, Tennessee 37218

Library of Congress Cataloging-in-Publication Data
Bonsall, Joseph S.
    Outside / by Joseph Bonsall ; illustrated by Erin Marie Mauterer. —
1st ed.
        p.   cm. — (A Molly book)
    Summary: When Molly sneaks out of a basement window she finds that
life as an outdoor cat is nothing like she had expected.
    ISBN 1-57102-130-2 (hc)
    [1. Cats—Fiction. 2. Lost and found possessions—Fiction.] I. Mauterer,
Erin, ill. II. Title. III. Series: Bonsall, Joseph S. Molly book.
    PZ7.B642750u 1998
    [E]—dc21   98-13303
                                                             CIP
                                                             AC

The illustrations in this book were rendered in watercolor, gouache, colored
    pencil, and acrylic.
The text type was set in ACaslon Regular.
The display type was set in ACaslon SwashBoldItalic and ACaslon BoldItalic.

First Edition

10 9 8 7 6 5 4 3 2 1

Alice: Can you tell me which path I should take?
Cheshire Cat: That depends a good deal on where you want to go!
Alice: I don't really know.
Cheshire Cat: Then, clearly, any path will do!

—Alice in Wonderland

Moral: If you're not sure where you're going, you're liable to end up someplace else — and not even know it.

Molly was sitting high up on her favorite lookout spot the first time she saw Spooker.

Molly's eyesight was young, and from up here she could see far down the hill. Every day she watched the Outside world go by from this very spot. Raccoons, squirrels, bunnies, Outside cats, and even other humancats (who were very entertaining) wandered by. And, every once in a while, the strangest of all the creatures would pass by — *DOGS!*

Molly sighed and stretched herself out, staring at the curious Outside world that was spread before her. It was then that she saw something coming up the long hill, walking slowly but surely right toward the Home!

Wow, thought Molly with a giggle, that *definitely* isn't *a dog*!

She watched in wonder as the handsome feline stranger walked right up to the screen door and peeked inside.

Now, Spooker was the color of a black tornado sky and had the biggest, roundest, greenest eyes Molly had ever seen. His fur was long, and he had a somewhat pushed-in nose. It was a mystery to Molly how it got that way.

Maybe he ran into a tree, she thought, *or maybe it was just like that from the day of his beginnings.*

Whatever the reason for his nose, this strange outdoor kitty created quite a stir when he showed up at the Home. Gypsy immediately jumped up and began hissing and growling right in the big face on the other side of the screen.

The stranger just yawned and, in the coolest catspeak Molly had ever heard, said, "Cool it, girl; you don't want to dirty those clean little paws, now do you?"

With that, Omaha ran for cover. He had several hiding places in the Home, and he sometimes hid so well that even Mother Mary couldn't find him.

Pumpkin padded softly over to the door and, in typical cat fashion, sat and stared straight into the eyes of the big outdoor cat. Gypsy backed down, but not much.

"What are you staring at, big guy? I'm not looking for trouble," said the black cat. "My name is Spooker."

"Okay, Spooker, what do you want?" asked Pumpkin.

"I want to meet the little one staring at me from up there. I think I know where she came from."

"Oh, no you don't!" spat Gypsy.

Molly could not believe what she had heard. Could this stranger really know something about her beginnings? Molly jumped down and cautiously approached the door. "Hello, Spook. I'm Molly," she said, feeling somewhat shy. "What do you know about me?"

"Well, first of all, the name is Spooker. Someday we really need to talk, but not today. I have to be going now," meowed the stranger as he started to walk away. "I'll be back around in a few days, so don't any of you get any hairballs caught in your throat," he laughed as he disappeared around the corner of the house.

Gypsy hissed. Pumpkin just stared thoughtfully. Omaha was still hidden. And as for little Molly, she was in love.

Several days had passed since Spooker's visit and Gypsy was worried. She sat high up on her favorite lookout spot. Gypsy was the self-appointed guardian of the Home, and the events of the last few days bothered her. All Molly talked about was Spooker, and Gypsy's kitty instincts were working overtime.

"That little girl is so young," Gypsy said to herself, "and so taken with this big, black furball. Molly wants to go Outside to find him, but she just doesn't realize how dangerous it is out there."

Gypsy jumped down and growled, "I am going to talk to that little girl right now!"

Gypsy searched all over the Home, but she could not find Molly. She became even more worried and went to talk to Omaha.

"Oh, no!" cried Omaha. "Where is she?"

"I was so afraid of this!" said Gypsy, shaking her head.

Old Pumpkin lowered his big orange head and sadly said, "She must have gone Outside."

"*Molly!*" screamed Mother Mary, staring at the open basement window.

Molly had snuck out the basement window! Molly was going to find Spooker!

She was an Outside cat, running through the grass and meowing with delight. This was wonderful! It was just like in her wildest dreams.

I'm going to find Spooker, and we are going to have a ball, she thought. *He will show me the Outside world!*

"MEEEEEOOOOOWWWWW!" she shouted happily.

It seemed to Molly that it had been days since she had snuck out of the Home, but in reality it had been just a few hours. Molly ran and ran until, almost without warning, the sky above began to darken. Suddenly the Outside became a very scary place. Molly slowly began to realize that she might be in serious trouble.

Oh, my, she thought. *I have really messed in my litter box this time! I am far from the Home, I have no idea where Spooker is, it's getting late, and I could be in danger!"*

Raindrops began to splash around her, and the darkness seemed to grow even blacker. The woods that had seemed like so much fun earlier now felt menacing. Molly wished that she were Home with her friends and Mother Mary. She hid in a patch of wild flowers and began to cry. She prayed to the God of All Creatures and asked him to watch over her and all who lived at the Home.

It was then that Molly heard the voice. It seemed to come from all around her. Molly had heard this same voice many times before, but before it had always spoken to her from the distant side of her dreams. But now the magical sound was right there with her, and it was the most beautiful catspeak that Molly had ever heard.

"Molly, my sweet, little Molly, do not cry. There is no need for you to worry. I am here to protect you."

"Who are you?" Molly stammered. "And where are you?"

"I am Angel," said the voice. "Sleep now, dear one, for I am watching. I am always watching over you."

The voice faded, and Molly curled herself into a tight little ball and fell into a deep sleep.

Omaha was simply beside himself with worry over little Molly. He was a little slower than the others. He didn't express himself as well as Pumpkin, he was not as brave as Gypsy, and he didn't have half the energy of Molly.

"But then, what cat in the whole world could compare to Molly?" sighed Omaha.

Ever since Molly had come into the Home, Omaha's life had never been the same. She was his best friend. And now the very worst thing had happened. Molly was gone!

"What are we gong to do, Pumpkin?' asked Omaha.

"I don't know what we *can* do," said Pumpkin, sounding very tired and sad. "But I do know that Mother Mary and Honey are out looking for her. We will just have to wait and pray to the mighty God of All Creatures that he will keep her safe and bring her back Home to us."

Omaha shook his head sadly, then padded off and curled up in Molly's bed. With his head on Molly's rainbow pillow, Omaha fell asleep as he prayed for Molly.

While Mother Mary and Honey searched for their little calico, Gypsy paced in front of the door. Her fur stood on end when she heard a now familiar voice come from the darkness outstide.

"Hey, you inside there, where's Molly?" purred the smooth voice of Spooker.

"How dare you come here!" Gypsy hissed. "You're the reason Molly is gone!"

"Gone? What are you talking about?" asked Spooker, concern creeping into his catspeak.

"I'm afraid that it's true," said Pumpkin, coming up behind Gypsy. "She left the Home this morning. No one knows where she is, but I believe she went looking for you!"

"That's right, and I'll make you pay for this!" threatened Gypsy.

"Everyone, please settle down. This is really serious!" said Omaha.

"The boy there is right. Perhaps I can help," said Spooker thoughtfully. "It is the least I can do. Believe me, I really meant no harm to her, no matter what that uppity feline may think."

Gypsy bristled.

"Would you help us, Spooker?" asked Pumpkin. "Please?" pleaded Omaha.

"Well, what about it?" huffed Gypsy. She didn't like this guy even a little, but she had to admit that they were quite helpless in the Home.

"I know the lands around here better than any cat alive," said the black cat as he turned away. "I'll find her!" Then, he was gone.

Spooker searched and searched, but with no luck. Then, he went to find the Dude.

The Dude was an old, white Outside cat who was as old as Pumpkin and even wiser. He had lived a hard life, and it showed. His fur was splotchy, half of his tail was gone (he took some kind of pride in the fact that a raccoon had bitten it off!), and his left eye was blind. This last he claimed was the result of a fight with an owl, although that story changed every other month.

The Dude was some piece of work, but Spooker knew the wise old cat could be trusted.

A better friend than an enemy, thought Spooker as he approached the huge stack of trash that the Dude called home.

"Hey there, Dude, are you home?" Spooker meowed. He always made sure that the Dude knew it was him from a ways off. He didn't want to *spook* the old guy, thought Spooker, chuckling to himself.

Spooker jumped a mile when the old Dude answered from directly behind him. "Hi there, fur boy! Juggle any mice lately?"

"Whoa, you scared me! I didn't even hear you sneak up," said the startled Spooker.

"Well, like I always say, 'That's being a cat!'" laughed the Dude, his catspeak fading in and out. "So, what brings you to this stack of rubble anyway?"

"I need your help," Spooker said, speaking slowly so as to be fully understood by the old warrior. "Are you familiar with the four uptown kitties who live indoors about three fields and some woods from here, over that way?" Spooker nodded toward the Home.

"Yeah," the Dude answered. "I know the place quite well. I used to stop by there regular like, for a little hand out. A cat can't be too proud when it comes to his stomach, you know. Why, there is a wonderful humancat there who loves kitties. And then there's Gypsy, and old Pumpkin, and that little fella — Omi or something . . ."

Spooker hated to interrupt, but the scrawny old cat might talk right up until the God of All Creatures came and took him to the Better Place — which by the looks of him could be any minute.

"Well, there is a young one also, a little girl kitty named Molly. She has run away, and I just have to find her," declared Spooker.

"I know of her," said the Dude. "I haven't been over that way for quite a while now, but word gets around. But it's gettin' too late to search for Molly tonight. She has surely found a place to hide by now, so let's rest, and we'll get started early in the morning." Spooker curled up reluctantly and tried to sleep. He hoped his friend could help him. Finally, among the old rags and blankets that the Dude called home, Spooker slept.

The next day, Molly awoke and realized that she must have slept in the flowers for a long time. Dawn was breaking and the forest was beginning to stir with new life — and new dangers.

Molly peeked out of the flowers and looked right into the face of a huge, muscular, reddish-colored cat. Her feline instincts warned her that she was in danger. She put out her claws and growled at the miserable looking thing before her, though deep inside she was scared to death!

Now, some creatures just have a bad streak — a natural meanness, or as old Pumpkin would say, "a darkness inside the heart." Red was one of those creatures — a nasty old outdoor kitty who had no friends as all. Oh, once in a while a few alley cat types from across the river would hang out with him, but even they would soon tire of his rotten attitude.

Most cats adjust to their lot in life, but not Red. Take the old Dude, for instance. A tough life had never turned him sour. He took every day as it came and always made the best of it.

The secret was "just being a cat!" according to the Dude, but most cats knew that there was much more to it than that. Cats were blessed creatures — a curious blend of intelligence, independence, agility, and curiosity. Above all, they had the God of All Creatures to look after them on the Earth and the promise of the Better Place.

As Molly stared at this dark-hearted, miserable wretch of a creature, Red attacked, scratching and biting at Molly. But Molly was quick on her feet. She backed away and took a swipe at the big cat. Her right front paw hit home just above Red's eye. He stood still for just a moment, both startled and surprised that this little kitty had actually hurt him. Then he began to hiss and spit. "I will get you!" he growled. "This is my territory, and I'll make you pay!"

Molly didn't waste any time. She ran as fast as she could with Red right on her tail, yowling and spitting. It was the most awful catspeak Molly had ever heard, and she believed that she would be going to the Better Place if this big, terrible cat were to catch her.

Red came closer and closer. Just as he was about to pounce on Molly, a big, black ball of fur slammed into the side of him.

Molly screeched to a halt and looked back over her shoulder. "Spooker!" she cried. "It's you!"

Molly could hardly believe what she was seeing and hearing. Spooker seemed to be everywhere at once, biting and clawing at Red. It was over quickly.

Red ran away, yelling and screaming, "I'll get all of you for this. Just you wait; you haven't heard the last of me!"

"Oh, blah, blah, blah," meowed another voice.

Molly turned and stared at the Dude.

"What happened to you?" she asked, staring at the battered white cat.

"Oh, just being a cat," answered the Dude, bowing slightly.

At that, Spooker, the Dude, and Molly laughed and laughed.

After the formal introductions were made, Spooker looked at Molly and said softly, "Let's go, girl. We're taking you Home."

It was early afternoon when Old Pumpkin saw Molly coming up the hill. He let out a joyful howl that brought everyone running to the back door.

"Molly, oh, my sweet Molly," exclaimed Mother Mary as she scooped up the little calico.

Omaha was meowing with delight; even Honey was jumping with joy. Gypsy walked over to the door and called out to Spooker and the Dude, who were already disappearing down the hill. "Thank you," she said solemnly. "Thank you for bringing Molly back to us."

After much celebration, Molly found herself alone at last with just her rainbow pillow and her pink mousie.

That really was quite an adventure! she thought. *Maybe next time, I can meet some more new friends.*

Molly then curled up and thanked the God of All Creatures for bringing her safely back to the Home. Angel looked down from the Better Place and smiled.